Broomsticks in Space

Kate Saunders worked as an actress until she was twenty-five and then became a writer. She has written five novels and edited a collection of short stories. As a journalist she has worked for the *Sunday Times*, the *Daily Telegraph*, the *Independent* and the *Sunday Express*, and is currently writing a weekly column in the *Express*. She can be heard regularly on BBC Radio 4, presenting *Woman's Hour* and appearing on *Start the Week* and *Front Row*. She lives in London and has a six-year-old son.

The *Belfry Witches* titles are Kate's first books for children. A major BBC TV series is based on them.

Titles in The Belfry Witches series

All Belfry Witches titles can be ordered at
your local bookshop or are available by post
from Book Service by Post (tel: 01624 675137).

The Belfry Witches
Broomsticks in Space

Kate Saunders
Illustrated by Tony Ross

MACMILLAN
CHILDREN'S BOOKS

For Bertie and Archie

First published 2000 by Macmillan Children's Books
a division of Macmillan Publishers Limited
25 Eccleston Place, London SW1W 9NF
Basingstoke and Oxford
www.macmillan.co.uk

Associated companies throughout the world

ISBN 0 330 37287 4

1 3 5 7 9 8 6 4 2

A CIP catalogue record for this book is available from
the British Library.

Typeset by SX Composing DTP, Rayleigh, Essex
Printed and bound in Great Britain by Mackays of Chatham plc, Kent

Contents

1

Marrow Madness

Skirty Marm landed her broomstick in the lane beside Blodge Farm and took a large, grubby piece of paper out of her hat. This was a list of names, and each name had a row of numbers beside it.

"Mrs Blenkinsop," read Skirty Marm. "Her marrow was forty-eight and a half centimetres, last time we looked. That's three whole centimetres bigger than ours."

Old Noshie had landed rather clumsily in the hedge. She struggled out of a clump of thorns. "Perhaps it's stopped growing," she said hopefully. "Perhaps it'll start shrinking soon, until it's just a tiny little courgette."

Once a week, all through this long, warm summer, the two witches had flown round the village of Tranters End, measuring every single vegetable marrow. There were no less than fifteen of these green monsters, lying in gardens and vegetable patches like vast, overgrown cucumbers. Marrows are not very exciting to eat, but the villagers were not growing them for food. They were all after the Marrow Cup – a silver cup, given every year at the Flower Show to the person who had raised the biggest marrow in Tranters End.

This year, for the first time, Old Noshie and Skirty Marm had entered the competition. They were both very proud of the fine, fat marrow they were growing in the vicarage garden. Old Noshie wanted to win that silver cup more than anything in the world. She lay awake at night, fretting over the sizes of all the other marrows in the village. Skirty Marm pretended not to care so much, but it had been her idea to measure their rivals' marrows.

Nobody in Tranters End was at all startled when they saw two determined witches flying from garden to garden with their tape-measure. Though it is far from usual to find two genuine witches, dressed in dusty rags and pointed hats, in a quiet English village, Old Noshie and Skirty Marm had become part of the scenery there. There had been some fuss when they first arrived, and several hair-raising magic incidents, but the villagers were now quite used to having a pair of witches living in the belfry of their church. They had even stopped thinking Old Noshie and Skirty Marm looked odd. Though of course, they did. Witches are not at all like humans – as you would know at once if you ever saw one. Their skin has a leathery toughness, and their hair is like the hard string used for tying parcels.

Old Noshie was a plump, bumbling sort of witch, with bright green skin that glowed in the dark. Her head was as bald as an egg, and she wore a blue wig to keep it warm. Skirty Marm was a skinny witch, with grey skin, purple hair, and red eyes that shot out sparks when she was angry.

The two witches had found Tranters End by mistake. It had happened nearly four years ago, at Hallowe'en. Old Noshie and Skirty Marm had been banished from Witch Island for singing a rude song about their wicked queen, Mrs Abercrombie. When they first came to the belfry, the two exiled witches had been very homesick. Nowadays they lived very happily underneath the deafening church bells.

Things had not always been so happy, however. For their first couple of years with the humans, Skirty and Noshie had been at war with the terrible MRS ABERCROMBIE. The ex-queen had done everything she could to destroy Old Noshie and Skirty Marm. She had plenty of reasons to hate them.

First, they had helped to bring about the Witch Island Revolution, which finally threw the evil queen off her throne.

Second (and worst of all), they had stolen the POWER HAT. This was an extraordinarily powerful witch's hat, two metres tall, with an everlasting candle burning at its point. Nobody knew all its secrets, but this Hat was the very heart of Mrs Abercrombie's power. Without it, she was nothing more than a very clever, very wicked and very ancient witch. With the Power Hat, she was the strongest witch in the world.

After Old Noshie and Skirty Marm stole the Hat, Mrs Abercrombie had laid all kinds of evil plans to snatch it back and had sworn never to rest until the Power Hat was hers once more.

In the end, the Power Hat had been Mrs Abercrombie's undoing. After one desperate battle it had burst into flames and vanished in a cloud of ash. Still Mrs Abercrombie refused to give in. She knew that before it had become a hat, this strange magic article had been a small piece of stone, with an eerie, silvery glow. Who should know better than Mrs Abercrombie, the very witch who had made the Hat? Yet again, she had refused to admit defeat. She had gone back in a Time Machine to capture the Glowing Stone and start all over again.

Then Skirty Marm had rescued the Glowing Stone and sent it hurtling away into outer space. Mrs Abercrombie had been so furious, she had EXPLODED. Her rage and disappointment blew her into a million pieces, and (like a wicked old witch at the end of a fairy story) she was never seen again.

All this had happened nearly a year ago. Since then, free from the looming shadow of Mrs A., the two witches had enjoyed the happiest, most peaceful year of their lives. As Old Noshie said: "I don't even see her disgusting face in my nightmares any more!"

Back on Witch Island, Old Noshie and Skirty Marm were national heroines for blowing up the evil ex-queen. If they had fancied it, they could have returned in triumph as two very important witches in the government (the witches' new leader, Chancellor Badsleeves, was an old friend of theirs). But they could not think of leaving their human friends in Tranters End. The greatest of these friends was the young curate, Mr Cuthbert Babbercorn. They also loved his sweet wife, Alice – who had once been turned into a snail by Mrs Abercrombie – and the Babbercorn baby, Thomas, who was their godson. Next to the Babbercorns, the witches loved Mr Snelling, the plump and kindly vicar. Before they came to Tranters End, Old Noshie and Skirty Marm had known nothing about human friendship, or human love – so much kinder and deeper than the witch version. Now that they did know about it, they could never live on Witch Island. Chancellor Badsleeves often complained that they had been "ruined" by soppy human ways.

Old Noshie and Skirty Marm liked these soppy ways and were proud to have so many friends in the village.

One of these called to them now, from the garden of his bungalow. "Afternoon, witches!" It was Mr Fisher, their friend from the Old Folks' Drop-In Club. "Is it measuring-day again?"

"Hello, Mr Fisher," said Old Noshie. "We're measuring a day early this week because we're off today."

Both witches made important-yet-modest faces, and Mr Fisher cried, "I nearly forgot! It's your special visit to Witch Island! Well, I hope you have a wonderful time."

Skirty Marm was worried. "Do you think our marrow will be all right while we're gone?"

Mr Fisher was not entering for the Marrow Cup this year, so he was free to give the witches advice. "It'll be fine as long as it has enough

7

water. The only things a marrow doesn't like are FROST and SNOW."

"Suppose there's a frost?" cried old Noshie in alarm.

Mr Fisher wanted to laugh, but politely turned it into a cough so he would not hurt the witches' feelings. "You won't get a frost in a lovely warm summer like this!"

Old Noshie and Skirty Marm had joined the Old Folks' Drop-In Club because they were over one hundred and fifty years old. This is very, very old for a human. But the kind and patient old people at the Club never forgot that one hundred and fifty is very, very young for a witch. Noshie and Skirty had also joined the Brownies, and felt quite at home playing and squabbling with the little girls.

Old Noshie squashed her green face between the slats of Mr Fisher's fence. "Everybody's marrow is bigger than ours. It's not fair. I do wish we could use just a tiny bit of magic!"

Skirty Marm snorted impatiently. "For the last time, you know we can't! If there's anything dodgy about our marrow, it'll be chucked right out of the Flower Show!"

"You know the rule," said Mr Fisher. "No

magic without Mr Babbercorn's permission."

"And he's never going to give us permission to CHEAT," said Skirty Marm. She sighed. There had been no major magic since the explosion of Mrs Abercrombie, and she could not help missing it a little. Skirty Marm had been top of her class at witch school, and winner of the Spellbinders' Medal for thirty-six years in a row. Mr Babbercorn allowed the witches to fly around the village on their brooms, and they occasionally cast very minor spells to unblock drains or mend fridges. But these were nothing to a witch who had once won the Transformation Cup by turning Old Noshie into a toadstool. Skirty Marm had to keep reminding herself that living without magic was better than living in fear of Mrs Abercrombie.

Old Noshie, always bottom of the class at school, had not missed magic nearly so much – until now. "Isn't there anything we can do to make our marrow grow?" she asked wistfully.

Mr Fisher kindly told them how to feed the marrow with sugared water and a piece of darning wool (he said this did not count as cheating), and added, "By the way – tell that Fancy-Pants talking cat to leave my roses alone!

I'm growing them for the Flower Show, not for Mr Mendax to give to his girlfriend!"

Old Noshie and Skirty Marm fell into a loud fit of giggles. Mendax was a talking cat who had been adopted by Mr Snelling. He had once been a cat-slave on Witch Island, sent by Mrs Abercrombie to spy on the witches. Though he was now a reformed character, the witches found it hard to forget his shady past. They thought it was very funny that this snooty, superior cat had fallen in love. Mendax had lost his heart to Gingersnap, the sister of the cat at the Post Office.

Skirty Marm sang, "Mendax and Gingersnap sitting in a tree – K-I-S-S-I-N-G!"

Old Noshie's marrow-fixated mind was already on the business of measuring. She led Skirty Marm through the gate of Blodge Farm and round the back of the large farmhouse to the vegetable patch. Mrs Blenkinsop's marrow lay under wire netting and looked depressingly enormous.

Old Noshie measured it, and her green lip wobbled. "Fifty centimetres!" she moaned.

Above them, a window flew open. From inside the house, Mrs Blenkinsop's voice

shouted, "Fifty-ONE centimetres, if you don't mind! You can measure all you like, but it won't stop my marrow winning the cup!" And she banged the window shut.

I'm very sorry to say that the two witches replied by sticking out their tongues and yelling, "BUM!"

Mr Babbercorn was beginning to worry that the Marrow Cup was not bringing out the best in the people of Tranters End. It had certainly not brought out the best in Old Noshie, usually such an easy-going witch. For the rest of that afternoon she got crosser and crosser as the rival marrows seemed to get bigger.

"Only six marrows smaller than ours," she said furiously when the measuring was over. "And Mrs Tucker's is a whole TWENTY centimetres bigger! It's not fair!"

Mrs Tucker kept the Post Office and General Shop and was also Brown Owl. The witches admired her very much, but Old Noshie was so jealous of the marrow that she wanted to spit on Mrs Tucker's washing – and she would have done, if Skirty Marm had not knocked her off her broomstick in the nick of time.

"I don't know what's got into you," Skirty said severely, when the two of them were back in their dusty belfry. "This is a very important day for us, and all you can think of is that stupid marrow!"

"The silver cup would look so great up here!" sighed Old Noshie. "I've cleared a special space for it, on top of my slug-box."

Skirty Marm gave her friend a quick biff on the nose to organize her thoughts. "Hurry up and get ready – we mustn't be late for the ceremony!"

The two witches and Mendax had been invited back to Witch Island for a Grand

Ceremony to honour them for the part they had played in Mrs Abercrombie's explosion.

"I wish they'd told us what sort of honour we're getting," said Old Noshie. "I hope it's a big FEAST!"

"You would," Skirty Marm said crushingly. "I'm hoping for a MEDAL. Or perhaps a TITLE – I've always fancied being a Dame of the Dustbin. Then I could sign my name 'Skirty Marm DD'."

Witches are not very tidy creatures, but Old Noshie and Skirty Marm made a special effort to look smart for this great occasion. Old Noshie polished her bald head before putting on her wig, and decorated her hat with a muddy lettuce. Skirty Marm felt very elegant in her new earrings, made of two old tea-strainers. They cleaned their broomsticks carefully and flew down to the vicarage garden.

Mr Babbercorn, Mr Snelling, Alice and Thomas were waiting to see them off. Mr Babbercorn held baby Thomas, and Alice held three paper bags.

"Just a snack to keep you going," she said, smiling. "Jam sandwiches for you two, and fish-paste for Mendax."

The vicar looked nervously at his watch. "Where is Mendax? That cat is always disappearing!"

"Here he comes," said Mr Babbercorn.

The small black cat strolled along the garden wall and dropped onto the lawn. He was humming to himself. His bright green eyes were dreamy, and there was a buttercup stuck in his collar. Old Noshie and Skirty Marm began giggling again.

"Am I late?" Mendax asked. "I was just saying goodbye to Gingersnap – sweet, artless little thing! How she blushed when she pressed this buttercup into my paw!"

"I dunno what you see in that cat," said Skirty Marm. "All she does is MEW!"

Mendax was offended. "I can still hold a conversation with ordinary cats, you know. And I find Gingersnap's innocence delightful. It does me so much good to talk to this simple village beauty and her honest brother!"

Mr Snelling bent down to kiss Mendax and to give him the small crash-helmet he had bought from a very expensive toy shop – the vicar spoiled his cat dreadfully. Mendax put on his helmet and settled in his basket on the back of Old Noshie's broomstick.

"Have a fantastic time, all of you!" said Mr Babbercorn. "You deserve to be honoured for your bravery." His eyes were very serious behind his glasses. "I know I can trust you to behave. Remember your promise to stay off the NASTY MEDICINE."

The witches looked rather sulky. As every human knows, it is STUPID and DANGEROUS to drink someone else's medicine, but for witches Nasty Medicine is a treat – all it does is make them disgustingly tipsy. Nasty Medicine

had got Old Noshie and Skirty Marm into all sorts of trouble in the past, but that did not stop them liking it.

"Couldn't we have just a little drop?" asked Skirty Marm. "Everyone else will be drinking – it'd be RUDE not to!"

"Absolutely not," Mr Babbercorn said firmly.

"You're supposed to be setting an example to the younger witches," Mr Snelling reminded them.

"Huh!" muttered Old Noshie. "They'll be too drunk to notice!"

Mr Babbercorn was a thin, pale, weedy young man – but he was the only person who could keep the witches in order. "I'm sorry, witches," he said, very kindly but very firmly. "No Nasty Medicine. Remember, you live with humans these days."

"Come home soon!" cried Alice. "Don't get so famous on Witch Island that you forget us!"

The witches could never do that. Their sulks melted away as they kissed and hugged the humans. Then, in the soft afternoon sunshine, they mounted their brooms.

2

Explosion Day

After two hours of hard flying (with a short break in Norway to eat their sandwiches), the witches and Mendax noticed a change in the air. It became colder, with a lashing wind and a dampness that seemed to seep into the marrow of their bones. The stormy sea was black beneath a threatening grey sky. The witches rammed their hats on tighter and put their brooms into second gear. Ahead of them, a black, jagged, sinister heap of rocks loomed through the mist.

Old Noshie and Skirty Marm cackled with delight. Although they had picked up many human tastes (for instance, electric light, decent biscuits) they still missed the ghastly weather of their old home.

"Mmmm, just SMELL it!" cried Skirty Marm as the familiar stink of bad eggs began to waft up from the rocks below.

Mendax, swinging giddily in his basket, shivered. His memories of Witch Island were not happy ones. In the dark days of Mrs Abercrombie, before slavery was made illegal, he had been a cat-slave. Many cats had been treated very cruelly, and Mendax had been beaten and starved by his drunken old owner.

The little cat forgot all this, however, when he saw the welcome that had been laid on for the Heroes of the Explosion. As the broomsticks circled above the palace beach, they all gasped.

A huge bonfire burned on the black sands. Hundreds of witches were crowded around it. As Old Noshie and Skirty Marm landed the brooms (careful not to squash anyone in the crowd) they were almost deafened by the loud cheers. Beneath this, they heard the deep and rasping notes of the Pock-horn – a witches' musical instrument, which looks rather like an enormous hot-water bottle made of metal. A group of witches held up a banner which said, "HAPPY EXPLOSION DAY, OLD NOSHIE AND SKIRTY MARM!" A group of former cat-slaves were chanting, "Men-DAX! Men-DAX! Men-DAX!"

"Dear me," murmured Mendax, wiping away a tear with his paw. "One is quite overwhelmed!"

A beaming, toothless witch pushed her way through the crowd.

"BINBAG!" yelled Old Noshie and Skirty Marm. Binbag was an old friend from school, and they were delighted to see her. Skirty Marm biffed Binbag's nose. Old Noshie knocked off Binbag's hat and jumped on it. Several witches nearby wept to see this touching reunion.

"This is our first National Explosion Day!" Binbag shouted, above the din. "We're going to have one every year – and it's all because of you!"

"Pooh, it was nothing!" mumbled Old Noshie, grinning and blushing dark green. Being hailed as a heroine was lovely and almost took her mind off the marrow.

The two witches and Mendax were escorted through the cheering crowd to the Meeting Cave, where the ceremony was to take place. Palace guards carried their broomsticks, Mendax's basket and the remaining sandwiches.

"Don't squash them," said Old Noshie. "I might fancy one later."

The Meeting Cave was a vast underground cavern, carved into the rock. It was packed with thousands and thousands of witches, all seated according to age and rank. I will quickly explain how you tell the age and importance of a witch. It's all in the STOCKINGS.

Up in the gallery of the Meeting Cave sat the YELLOW-STOCKINGS. These are baby witches, under the age of one hundred and still at school. In front of them were the young RED-STOCKINGS, who were between the ages of one hundred and two hundred – Old Noshie and Skirty Marm were Red-Stockings.

The front rows of the Meeting Cave were divided into two blocks. On the left-hand side sat the GREEN-STOCKINGS – that is, witches between the ages of two hundred and three hundred. On the right side sat the oldest and most powerful witches of all, the PURPLE-STOCKINGS.

Some of these witches were very old indeed. Mrs Abercrombie had been nearly a thousand, and though she had been one of the cleverest witches, she was not the oldest. Purple-Stockings are the kind of witches you read about in fairy stories. If you ever have a nightmare about a wicked witch, ten to one she'll be wearing purple stockings.

Under Mrs Abercrombie's evil rule, the old Purples kept cat-slaves and bullied the younger witches. The Revolution had changed all that by chucking out the queen and electing a popular Red-Stocking government. Nowadays, the Purples had far less power, and they were always grumbling about "fancy new-fangled ways". They did not think the Explosion of Mrs Abercrombie was a reason for celebration, and they were the only witches who did not cheer when Old Noshie and Skirty Marm were led on to the platform in the Meeting Cave.

It was very strange for Old Noshie and Skirty Marm. The last time they had stood in this cave, with everyone staring at them, they had been prisoners. Mrs Abercrombie had found them guilty of treason for singing the disgracefully rude song about her. She had stripped away their red stockings and banished them for a hundred years. Who could have imagined, on that terrible day, that the two disgraced witches would return in triumph?

There was a loud Pock-horn fanfare, and Chancellor Badsleeves entered. She was a stout witch, with short white hair and round glasses. Since the overthrow of Mrs Abercrombie, she had been the Chancellor of Witch Island. She was an old friend of Old Noshie and Skirty Marm's (she had lived in the cave next door), and she gave them a beaming smile as she held up her hand for silence. A hush fell upon the great Cave.

"Fellow-witches," said Badsleeves, "we are gathered here today to honour the three citizens who gave us EXPLOSION DAY. These two witches, and this cat, have beaten Mrs Abercrombie again and again. On the last occasion they sent the Glowing Stone into outer space, where the nasty old bag couldn't get her hands on it. They made her so furious, she Exploded. It is my great pleasure to reward them with the highest honours of our Island."

There was another Pock-horn fanfare. A Purple-Stocking palace guard brought in a ragged black cushion. Chancellor Badsleeves picked up a small medal, on a short silk ribbon.

"Step forward, MENDAX!"

Mendax stepped forward on shaking paws and bowed to the Chancellor. The freed cat-slaves, sitting at the front and sides of the cave, burst into ear-splitting mews.

"Mendax, for your bravery I hereby make you a KNIGHT OF THE NEWT." She hung the medal round his neck. "Arise, Sir Mendax, KN."

This ancient honour had never been given to a cat before. In their pride and joy, the cats began to swarm and shriek. Mendax was, for once, speechless. He gaped at the cheering cats, posed for photographs with the Chancellor, and slunk to the back of the platform in a state of shock. This was more wonderful than his

wildest dreams. In Latin (as Mr Snelling loved to point out), "Mendax" means "Liar", and this cat did tell some thumping lies – even he would never have dared to lie on such a magnificent scale as this.

Skirty Marm nudged Old Noshie excitedly. If Mendax was a Knight of the Newt, what did Badsleeves have in store for them?

"Step forward, OLD NOSHIE and SKIRTY MARM!"

The two witches stepped forward, feeling very awkward, and bowed to Badsleeves. The lettuce on Old Noshie's hat fell off and hit the Chancellor's foot.

"Noshie and Skirty," said Badsleeves, forgetting to be grand, "you outwitted Mrs Abercrombie until the old horror got so mad she Exploded. We can't thank you enough, and we're making you Dames of the Dustbin. But you expected that. We thought you deserved something extra – and then we remembered that Mrs A. had stripped you of your STOCKINGS."

Old Noshie and Skirty Marm turned pale. Could they be getting their stockings back at last? Mrs Tucker had kindly knitted them replacements (which they were wearing now), but these were not the same. Real witch-stockings are very tough, almost like boots.

Badsleeves grinned. "I'm not going to give you back your red stockings. I'm going to replace them – with these!"

From the ragged cushion, she picked up two new pairs of GREEN STOCKINGS.

This was a sensation. It had never happened before, in the whole history of Witch Island – an early Promotion, which would give two young Red-Stockings all the powers and privileges of Greens. The reporters in the Press Gallery were going crazy, and the crowd (apart from one or two sour old Purples) was cheering itself hoarse.

Old Noshie and Skirty Marm took off Mrs Tucker's red stockings, and dazedly pulled on the new green stockings.

"Is this a dream?" asked Old Noshie.

"We're GREENS!" cried Skirty Marm gleefully. "We can park our brooms in the palace railings and drop litter!"

It was a huge honour. After the ceremony, the witches and Mendax were hemmed in by admirers. Mendax was dragged away to a cat-party in one of the old slave tunnels. Witches of every stocking-colour queued to congratulate the new Greens. Over and over again, people told them they were saviours and heroes and wonderful and marvellous – until Old Noshie and Skirty Marm started to believe it. Tranters End seemed very far away. Mr Babbercorn and Mr Snelling did not call them wonderful or marvellous. What did they know? How could mere humans understand?

"Let's have some Nasty Medicine," said Skirty Marm.

"Just what a witch needs after a shock like that," agreed Old Noshie.

"After all, we're not little Red-Stockings any more," said Skirty Marm. "Us GREENS are old enough to handle anything!"

At the State Banquet which followed the ceremony, Old Noshie and Skirty Marm each drank a whole bottle of Nasty Medicine. So did their old pal, Chancellor Badsleeves. I am sorry to say that they were all revoltingly tipsy.

When the clocks struck midnight, Badsleeves burst into tears and cried, "You're the besh frenge a wisht heverad—!" and then collapsed into a bowl of spider trifle, snoring loudly.

"Deary me," hiccupped Old Noshie,

"perhaps we'd better go home."

"Pooh to that!" sang Skirty Marm. "The night is YOUNG!" She picked up two more bottles of Nasty Medicine. "Let's sneak away from this boring banquet, and visit some of our old haunts!"

The "Cough and Spit" was a Red-Stocking drinking cellar. When Old Noshie and Skirty Marm rolled in, all their old friends were waiting to cheer them. They sat down with Binbag, and her cave-mate Moonbott, and chatted about old times.

Suddenly, Skirty Marm gave Old Noshie a sharp nudge. "Look over there!"

She pointed to a large table in the corner. Around it, six witches were playing SQUITBLAT. This was a popular gambling game, played with cards and stone counters – and Skirty Marm had always fancied herself as a bit of a Squitblat expert. Mr Babbercorn, who hated gambling, would have been horrified to see the two witches joining the game. He would have been even more horrified to see them ordering several more bottles of Nasty Medicine.

Skirty Marm was good at Squitblat, so Old Noshie was not surprised to see her winning a pile of stone witch-money. The surprise was Old Noshie, who had never won a game of Squitblat in her life. Today, she could not stop winning. Very proud of herself, she scooped all the money into a small sack.

"I'm a RICH WITCH," Old Noshie said, with a giggle. "Well, I'm off now, Skirty. I'm getting some fresh air, some grub and another bottle of medicine. Coming?"

"No," said Skirty Marm, deep in her cards.

So Old Noshie went off exploring by herself. Normally, she would have been too timid to explore without Skirty Marm, but the Nasty Medicine had given her a false and foolish courage. If only she had been sober, she would have remembered how risky it was to visit the docks after dark. The Witch Island Docks were the roughest place on the Island – noisy, smelly, crowded and full of thieves and murderers.

With no very clear idea in her fuddled head of how she had got there, Old Noshie gaped around her. Gangs of sailor-witches, covered with tattoos, pushed past her in the narrow streets. The great wooden masts of the ships towered above a jumble of black rooftops. A fight was starting on the other side of the street. Old Noshie wanted to get away from the pushing and shouting. She stumbled through a door with a faded sign above it that said, *The Gastric Ulcer – Bar Snacks – Medicines*.

She was in a low sailors' tavern, very dark and full of smoke. The only customers appeared to be two very dirty, wrinkled old witches. One wore a black patch over one eye; the other had a hook instead of a hand. Both were smoking pipes. When these two witches saw Old Noshie, they stopped talking. The witch with the eyepatch hastily hid something in her lap.

Old Noshie was not a brave witch, and she did not like the look of these two characters. But there was a stout bottle of Nasty Medicine on the table between them, and she did like the look of that.

"Well, well!" chortled the Eyepatch witch, her one eye gleaming. "If it ain't Old Noshie, the National Heroine! Do two old sailors an honour and have a drink with us!"

Old Noshie wasn't sure, but thought one little drink could not do any harm. After four little drinks, she had decided that the two old sailors were her favourite witches in the world. She insisted on buying them another bottle of Nasty Medicine. The sailors licked their lips greedily when she produced the little sack full of her Squitblat winnings.

They began to ask Old Noshie all kinds of searching questions about herself. It was not long before Old Noshie began to talk about marrows. Eyepatch said it was a dreadful shame her marrow wouldn't grow.

"You know, Noshie," Eyepatch said, "you should use a spot of magic!"

Old Noshie shook her head. "I can't. Our curate has got ever so good at recognizing all the OBVIOUS sorts of magic."

"Then it's a very good thing you ran into me and my mate," Eyepatch said. "We've got a spell your curate-bloke will never notice – it's not obvious magic, by any means." She winked hard with her single eye. "We're in a bit of a hurry to get rid of it. Our ship sails tonight, and we don't want it to fall into the wrong hands."

Old Noshie was not a quick-witted witch, but she understood that Eyepatch wanted to sell her a black-market spell.

Eyepatch, cackling wickedly, pulled a small velvet bag from her rags. "Take a look at this, Noshie. It's the very latest in Growing-charms! A friend of ours stole – ahem! – BORROWED it from a research lab at the University."

Old Noshie stared fearfully at the bag. Buying or selling illegal spells was a very serious crime on Witch Island. And Mr Babbercorn was bound to disapprove. But she couldn't help thinking how splendid it would be to collect the silver cup for the prize marrow. If nobody would be able to tell she had used magic, where was the harm?

"This will make anything grow," whispered Eyepatch into Old Noshie's guilty green ear. "As much or as little as you want. Have a look!" She gave the velvet bag to Old Noshie.

On Witch Island, valuable spells and charms are often made of precious stones, and beautifully carved.

Old Noshie carefully took out the Growing-charm. It was about the size and shape of a hens' egg, completely covered in emeralds. Between the rows of jewels, in tiny writing, were the instructions for using the charm with a standard Biggening spell.

"Pretty, ain't it?" asked Eyepatch, taking it back. She nudged her friend, and the witch with the hook grunted. "Worth a small fortune, that is."

"I haven't got a fortune," said Old Noshie.

The sailor-witches laughed, in a way that was rather horrible. Old Noshie tried to join in, but her voice came out high and wobbly.

"What you've got in your purse will do," said Eyepatch.

She grabbed Old Noshie's sack of money and dropped the stolen charm into her lap.

The two sailor-witches stood up.

"Wait!" cried Old Noshie. "How do I know this thing's not DANGEROUS?"

"Ha ha! You DON'T!" screeched Eyepatch.

And both witches suddenly vanished into thin air.

3

A Cold Spell

Old Noshie woke up next morning feeling terrible. She was lying in a gutter near the palace, with no idea how she had got there.

"How could I have been so stupid?" she moaned to herself. "Why did I drink all that Nasty Medicine? Deary me – I'll never touch another drop again!"

All at once, the memory of last night came rushing back to her, and she shuddered. It was incredible – she could hardly believe it. Easygoing, timid Old Noshie had played Squitblat, skulked around the docks, and bought a black-market charm from two sailor-witches. If Mr Babbercorn ever found out, he would be scandalized.

Old Noshie was deeply ashamed of herself. She felt in her pocket for the stolen charm. Yes, it was still there. She knew she ought to take it straight to the police – and then into her mind popped a vision of her marrow.

She saw it, green and plump, wearing a red rosette that said "1st Prize". She saw it surrounded by admiring humans. She couldn't wait to tell Skirty Marm – that silver cup was as good as won. Smiling to herself, Old Noshie tucked the charm into the secret pocket inside her vest and strolled into the palace to find her friends.

The palace was in a dreadful mess after last night's party – littered with bat-bones, empty medicine bottles and snoring witches. Mendax and Skirty Marm were in the old throne-room, sipping cups of warm rainwater.

"Morning!" beamed Old Noshie. "Blimey, Skirty – where are your clothes?"

Skirty Marm was wearing nothing but her new stockings, a pair of long bloomers and a vest.

"I lost everything at Squitblat," Skirty Marm said gloomily. "I would have lost these bloomers, too, if the police hadn't raided the cellar and stopped the game."

Mendax shuddered. His eyes were hidden by dark glasses. "This place is so SORDID! Thank

goodness Miss Binbag offered to fetch you some more rags – because I refuse to fly home with a half-naked witch!"

"I had a brill time last night," Old Noshie said. She nodded in a meaningful way at Skirty Marm to show she had a secret to tell.

"Stop pulling silly faces at me!" snapped Skirty Marm. "Mr Babbercorn was right, and I should have listened to him. Gambling is a STUPID way to lose your money. Nasty Medicine gives you nothing but a big headache. From now on, I'm going to be good all the time."

Old Noshie was alarmed. "ALL the time?"

"Yes," Skirty Marm said firmly. "No more wild witch parties. No more magic."

"No magic!" squeaked Old Noshie. This could be tricky. Skirty Marm being good meant no help with the charm – and Noshie was not at all sure she could make it work on her own.

"What's the matter?" asked Skirty Marm.

"Nothing!" said Old Noshie, feeling her pocket nervously. Her green face blushed the colour of a Savoy cabbage.

Skirty Marm did not notice how shifty Old Noshie looked, because Binbag arrived at that moment with the spare clothes. Skirty Marm put them on with a lot of grumbling about the quality of the material. The ragged dress was skimpy and showed too much bloomer, but the hat was in the latest fashion (wide brim, narrow point) and rather smart. Skirty Marm studied her reflection for a long time and tried the hat at several angles until Mendax spat, "Is this a fashion show? I want to go home!"

Skirty tore herself away from the mirror, and the two witches and Mendax made their way down to the palace beach. A large crowd had gathered to see them off, but there was no more cheering. Every witch on the Island was feeling fragile after the celebrations. This crowd was so quiet you could hear every rasping note of the Pock-horn band.

The Chancellor (with a bag of ice under her hat to soothe her sore head) solemnly smacked them all goodbye. Mendax fitted on his miniature crash helmet and climbed into his basket. The witches mounted their brooms.

"Goodbye!" called Chancellor Badsleeves. "Come back for Explosion Day next year!"

The Pock-horn band played, "Will ye no come back again?" The two brooms leapt up into the grey air and shot out over the sea.

Skirty Marm and Old Noshie perked up when the smells of an English summer wafted through the warm air. Witch Island had been fun, but they were longing for the peace and quiet of home.

Mendax took off his dark glasses. "Ah, my beloved! I shall lay all my honours at her little ginger feet! What do I care for prizes if they do not please fair Gingersnap?"

"I can't wait to see Mr B.—" began Old Noshie, then stopped suddenly. How could she face Mr Babbercorn when she was planning to do something wicked?

All the Babbercorns and Mr Snelling rushed out of the vicarage as soon as the two brooms landed on the lawn. Beaming with pride and happiness, the three heroes gabbled out the news about their amazing honours. The vicar was delighted to have a titled cat.

"When you get married, your wife will be LADY MENDAX!" he giggled. "How splendid!"

"Mr Snelling – spare my blushes!" Mendax murmured. "I haven't asked her yet!"

Mr Babbercorn and Alice were very impressed by the witches' new green stockings.

"This shows that the other witches respect you," said Mr Babbercorn. "They trust you not to do anything dodgy!"

He meant it as a joke, but his words were torture to guilty Old Noshie.

"I can't go through with it!" she thought miserably. "I'll tell Mr B. everything!"

But she thought she would slip out and take a look at her marrow first.

There it lay, green and gleaming, in its soft bed of soil. But when Old Noshie measured it, she

39

was dismayed to find it had not grown a single millimetre. Very slowly, with a thumping heart, she pulled the stolen spell out of her vest. The emeralds winked in the warm afternoon sunshine.

Old Noshie could not resist. She adjusted her eyes to read the tiny writing (witches can improve their eyesight by pulling their ears) and did her best to take in the instructions. It was easier than she had expected. The magic part of the charm was stored in the form of a mist inside the egg-shaped case. It could be released by a

gentle squeeze of the hand, while reciting the standard Biggening Spell.

Old Noshie's only problem was remembering the standard spell.

"Drat – I wish I could talk to Skirty Marm," she thought. "She'd know how to do it!"

"Noshie!" Alice's voice called, across the garden. "Tea's ready!"

"Coming!" gasped Old Noshie. In a panic, she gabbled what she hoped was the spell and squeezed the charm above the marrow. The charm turned warm against her hand, then icy cold. A wisp of green smoke swirled over the flower bed for a moment, and vanished.

"Right," said Old Noshie, frowning at the marrow. "Start growing!"

Biting, freezing cold woke the witches in the belfry next morning. Their noses were frozen, the bells were hung with icicles. The world outside lay under a thick white blanket of snow.

"Brrrr!" said Skirty Marm. "What's going on?"

Her teeth chattering, she went over to one of the big windows.

"You don't get snow in JUNE!" said Skirty Marm.

Old Noshie jumped out of bed. "Skirty – the marrow! Mr Fisher said they don't like the cold!"

The witches leapt on their broomsticks and swooped down to the snowy vicarage garden. To their huge relief, their marrow looked as healthy and glossy as ever. Skirty Marm went into the house to borrow one of Thomas's baby-blankets to wrap around the marrow. While she was gone, Old Noshie measured the big green vegetable. She was terribly disappointed to find that it had not grown.

"Perhaps," she whispered hopefully to herself, "it takes a couple of days to work."

At least her precious marrow had not suffered in the freakish weather. The cold weather had attacked strawberries, roses and geraniums like knives. Nobody could explain it, and when the villagers found that the snow was only over Tranters End (it stopped at the boundaries of St Tranter's parish), they could not help suspecting the witches. How else could you explain snow in June?

Mr Babbercorn spent the whole day assuring

people that Old Noshie and Skirty Marm were completely innocent. "They'd never do anything to harm their marrow," he pointed out. "And they don't get up to that sort of mischief any more."

Privately, he begged the witches to confess if they had been mucking about with the weather.

"Mucking about?" cried Skirty Marm. "Us? Never!"

"Never!" echoed Old Noshie.

"We haven't performed a single spell since we came home," Skirty went on. "Have we, Nosh?"

"Oh, I believe you," Mr Babbercorn said happily. "And I'm so proud of you for giving up your witchy ways!"

Neither he nor Skirty Marm noticed that Old Noshie's green face had gone as pale as a peppermint cream.

4

Deep Trouble

The freakish weather continued through the next day. The people of Tranters End turned on their central heating and took out their thick winter jumpers. Although Mr Babbercorn did his best to proclaim the innocence of the witches, a cloud of suspicion still hung over them. This made Skirty Marm very indignant, and Old Noshie very shifty. She had begun to wonder if the frost could have anything to do with her black-market spell.

On the evening of the second day, as the sky darkened, a new light was noticed high in the night sky. This time, it was not only above Tranters End – there was something about the strange new star on the television news.

Next morning, Mr Snelling woke before dawn with a feeling that something was NOT RIGHT. First, he realized that his nose was no longer frozen, which meant that the snow had gone and the temperature was back to normal. Second – far more shocking – Mendax's basket was empty. His tartan cat-duvet and tiny hot-water bottle lay just where the doting vicar had placed them the night before. He had not come home!

In a sudden panic, Mr Snelling pulled on his dressing gown and rushed outside into the grey half-light.

"Mendax!" he called. "Are you there? OW!" The ground fell away under the vicar's slippers. He rolled over and over until he found himself lying at the bottom of an enormous hole which had appeared in the vicarage lawn. The hole looked as if something as big as a house had burst out of it.

Mr Snelling's shouts of "Help! Help!" woke the Babbercorns and the witches. They all ran out into the garden and gaped in astonishment at the gigantic, yawning crater. How had this happened?

Old Noshie checked her marrow and was relieved to find it as healthy as ever, right on the edge of the hole. Mr Snelling looked very small down at the bottom of the deep pit, and he could not get out until Mr Babbercorn had fetched a long ladder.

"I'd better report this to PC Bloater," Mr Babbercorn said, in a worried voice. "It's certainly very odd. Witches—" He was very solemn. "You can tell me the truth, and I won't be angry. Have you been doing magic behind my back?"

"No!" cried Skirty Marm.

"No," mumbled Old Noshie, with her fingers and toes crossed. Now she was sure that all this upheaval must have been caused by her stolen spell, and she was suffering agonies of guilt.

"There must have been a tremendous explosion," said Mr Snelling, brushing soil from his dressing gown. "I wonder why none of us heard it?" A dreadful thought struck him. "Oh, witches – do you think Mendax could have been blown up?"

Skirty Marm did not like to see the kind vicar so worried. "Rubbish," she said stoutly. "That cat hasn't just got nine lives – he's got at least NINETY! Leave it to us – we'll soon find him! Won't we, Noshie?"

"Mmm-nnn-m," mumbled Old Noshie.

The moment it was properly light, the two

witches went down to the post office. It was not open yet, but Boots – the fat brother of Gingersnap, Mendax's girlfriend – was lying in a patch of sun on the windowsill.

"Good morning, Boots," Old Noshie said (witches can speak the language of any animal). "Have you seen Mendax?"

Boots slowly opened one cross green eye. "No," he said, in his deep, snarling mew. "And I don't want to see him. He shouldn't have come here – making eyes at my sister and turning her head with his fancy ways! Too good for us now, she is!"

"Go on, Boots," Skirty Marm said. "Be a sport. There's a kipper in it for you!"

Boots thought for a moment. Then he said, "All right. A WHOLE kipper, mind! Your pal Mendax had a quarrel with Gingersnap last night and rushed off saying all was at an end. Dunno where."

"I can guess," Skirty Marm said, relieved. "He'll be hiding in his Sulking Tree."

Mendax's Sulking Tree was a tall old oak, in the woods behind the church. Mr Snelling was not supposed to know that Mendax hid at the very top of this tree whenever he wanted to be alone.

"I'm very glad you told me," Mr Snelling said to the witches, at the bottom of the tree. "If he's broken up with Gingersnap, he needs me." He sighed. "Such a pity – I was looking forward to him having a wife and kittens!"

The roly-poly vicar was not fond of flying, but there was no other way to get him to the top of the Sulking Tree. Old Noshie and Skirty Marm stuck their brooms under his arms and flew him up to the highest branch.

At first, Mendax shouted, "Go away! Leave me alone to die of my broken heart!"

But as the vicar came nearer, he started to fuss. "Careful – he'll fall! Hold tight, Mr Snelling!"

The witches hauled Mr Snelling up on to the branch beside Mendax, and the heartbroken cat could not help jumping into the vicar's arms.

"It's all over!" he cried. "I asked Gingersnap to marry me – and she REFUSED!"

"Maybe she's found another cat," suggested Skirty Marm.

"She has NOT!" Mendax spat crossly, his whiskers bristling. "She says she can't marry me because I'm too far above her – I can talk

like a human, and she can only mew. She won't believe me when I say I love her just as she is!" He groaned. "I must learn to live without her. I may travel or take up some missionary work. If I can't live for Gingersnap, I must live for others!"

Mr Snelling blew his nose. He was deeply touched by his cat's goodness and bravery. "Witches, could you carry us down, please? This branch doesn't feel very safe."

Mr Snelling led the way back to the vicarage, holding his lovesick cat in his arms. "Hello!" he called, stepping through the back door into the kitchen. "I've found him!"

The kitchen was empty, and the house was strangely quiet.

"Hello!" he called again. "Cuthbert? Alice?"

After more silence, Alice's voice came from the sitting room. "We're in here!" She sounded odd – not exactly scared, but nervous.

Mr Snelling went into the sitting room and gasped, "Great Scott!"

At first glance, it looked as if someone had dumped a pile of rubbish in the middle of the sofa. At second glance, this turned out to be a witch – extremely ragged, and very, very old. Her ancient cloak and pointed hat were covered in cobwebs, and moths were fluttering around a battered carpet-bag at her feet.

"Professor Mouldypage!" cried the witches. She was the last person they had expected to see.

This ancient witch was the State Librarian of Witch Island, and a great scholar. Her knowledge of magic was immense. She was the only living witch who knew more about the Power Hat than Mrs Abercrombie had – and also the only witch who had been able to strike fear into Mrs Abercrombie's black heart.

The professor had visited Tranters End before.

"What a nice surprise," said the vicar politely, once he had recovered from the shock of finding the peculiar old witch on his sofa.

"She won't say a word to us," said Mr Babbercorn. "She's been waiting for Old Noshie and Skirty Marm."

Little Thomas was sitting on his lap. Thomas had grown into a toddler now, but he still used the language called "Babyspeak", which the witches could understand.

"Be careful," Thomas warned, in Babyspeak. "You two are in DEEP TROUBLE!"

Skirty Marm laughed. "Who, US? We're National Heroines! Dames of the Dustbin don't get into trouble!"

Professor Mouldypage raised her hand and pointed her gnarled old finger at Skirty Marm. "Insolent young witch," she croaked, in her rusty, creaking old voice. "The human child is right – you're in the deepest trouble of your lives! You could be stripped of your new green stockings for this!"

"Eh?" Skirty Marm was alarmed now. "What are you talking about?"

"You can hide nothing from me and my magical charts," said Mouldypage. "I know that someone here has used powerful magic to do a HORRIBLE thing. I have seen the signs of MRS ABERCROMBIE in the night sky!" She sniffed crossly. "In short, some dratted fool has managed to bring her back to life!"

This was a bombshell. Both witches turned deathly pale. Could this appalling news be true?

"Don't try to deny it," croaked Mouldypage. "I've been getting the signs on my radar since the day before yesterday. Someone has REBUILT Mrs Abercrombie, and the magic came from HERE!"

"Well, you're WRONG," Skirty Marm shouted furiously. "We haven't touched any magic – have we, Nosh?"

Old Noshie was trembling. "N-n-n—" she stammered.

"Come on, Professor!" protested Mr Babbercorn, trying to sound brave. "Mrs Abercrombie exploded into a million pieces! We all saw it. These two witches aren't nearly clever enough to put all that together!"

"Not on their own," said Mouldypage. She had very sharp black eyes among her wrinkles, and she pinned these on Old Noshie. "While you were visiting the Island, a valuable spell was stolen from a research-cave at the University. It was a spell designed not just to grow things, but to RE-GROW them too – from even the tiniest fragment."

"Noshie, what's the matter?" cried Alice, alarmed at Old Noshie's paleness and trembling. "Are you ill?"

The guilty green witch could stand it no longer. "All right!" she shouted, bursting into tears. "I did it! But they told me it was just a growing-spell people couldn't see! And I only put a little drop on my marrow!"

"You did WHAT?" shrieked Skirty Marm. "You old fool – there must have been bits of Mrs A. all over the garden! You've grown her instead!"

"I suppose that explains the funny weather," said Mr Snelling. "And the huge hole in the garden. It must be general upheaval due to vast and enormous magic."

"And it explains the new light in the sky," said Professor Mouldypage. "All my charts and instruments tell me that's none other than Mrs Abercrombie herself – alive and well and combing the Galaxy for the Glowing Stone! If she catches it, and turns it back into her Power Hat, we're all DOOMED!"

Witches, humans and cat went very quiet as they digested this terrible piece of news.

"It's all my fault!" sobbed Old Noshie. "I wanted to win the Marrow Cup, and instead I've brought Mrs A. back to life. Oh, Skirt – you'd better kill me!"

"Don't be silly," Skirty Marm said crossly. "Stop snivelling."

Mr Snelling stroked Mendax's warm black fur. "There must be something we can do."

"Absolutely nothing," rasped Mouldypage calmly. "Unless you go into outer space and catch that Glowing Stone before she does."

Skirty Marm stood up very straight and held her head high. "Then that's what we'll do!" she said proudly. "Noshie's a stupid old basket – but we're still a TEAM."

Old Noshie wiped her nose on her hat. "Thanks, Skirty."

Mendax leapt out of the vicar's arms. "I'd like to volunteer for the suicide mission too. What does it matter if I never come back?"

To everyone's surprise, the deep wrinkles of

Mouldypage's face squidged into what looked like a smile. "I thought you'd both stick with the idiotic green one, so I decided to give you one last chance. I haven't reported you to the Witch Police – I haven't even told anyone on the Island what I've seen in the skies. If you three can defeat Mrs Abercrombie one more time, nobody will ever know."

It was a very small chance, and it would involve the witches and Mendax in terrible danger, but Skirty Marm grabbed at it gratefully. "We're not disgraced yet! We still have our new green stockings! Now we can prove we're WORTHY of them!"

In the vicar's study (with the blinds drawn in case of enemy spies), Old Noshie and Skirty Marm adapted their broomsticks for space-travel, giving them extra super-strength so they would not break up when they went through the atmosphere. Mouldypage mixed an evil-tasting potion, which would have the same strengthening effect on the witches and Mendax.

Mouldypage then muttered a spell that gave Old Noshie and Skirty Marm flaps of extra skin on their necks, like the gills of a fish. With these, they would be able to breathe in space. For Mendax, she made a special backpack of oxygen and a space helmet that had once been the vicar's goldfish bowl.

By nightfall, everything was ready for the voyage. Alice, Mr Babbercorn and Mr Snelling were very afraid they would never see their magic friends again – the strange new light in the sky looked very sinister – but they did their best to be very cheerful and brave. They followed the witches and Mendax out into the dark garden and stood well back as the rocket-brooms took off in a great burst of flame.

"Good luck!" they cried. "Come back soon!"

Skirty Marm had been worried that she would cry, but she was too busy clinging to her broomstick. It shot upwards through the air like an arrow, gathering speed until she could hardly breathe. She felt a huge jolt and shudder as they went through the Earth's atmosphere – and then, suddenly, the roar in her ears turned to the deepest silence she had ever heard. Her broom had slowed down. Old Noshie's broom bobbed along beside her. They all stared, with open mouths, at the wonderful sights around them.

Planet Earth, and our moon, were far behind

them. They were drifting through a vast, humming blackness, where stars, planets and meteors sparkled like jewels. It was very cold. It did not feel as if they were travelling fast, but the stars fell away behind them with remarkable speed.

"Goodness, that was Pluto," said Mendax, his voice echoing in the vast emptiness. "We're heading out of our solar system – I hope someone remembers the way home!"

They were heading towards the sinister new light, where Mouldypage's runes and spells had said Mrs Abercrombie was to be found. This light, shining from a small new planet, was very bright – but there was something unsavoury about it, like the air around a bad fish.

For endless hours they flew through rocks and stars and clouds of glittering dust and never seemed to get any nearer. At last, they were close enough to plunge their broomsticks headlong into the planet's damp grey atmosphere.

"Hang on!" yelled Skirty Marm.

The two brooms shot through the atmosphere of this mysterious new planet and landed in a heap on something squashy.

5

Deep Space

The black ground was slightly sticky, slightly warm and very dirty.

"Yuck, what a stinky place!" said Skirty Marm. "No wonder Mrs Abercrombie chose it."

Old Noshie tried to sound casual, but her voice wobbled. "I – I wonder where she is?"

"We should be careful," Mendax said. "She might be watching us."

Skirty Marm stuck her broom into the soft ground. There was a loud rumble of thunder and the ground suddenly gave a great, shuddering heave, which flung the witches and Mendax right off their feet.

"Rather a BOUNCY place," remarked Mendax, steadying himself with his tail.

The strange, bouncy, wobbly ground stopped heaving. Skirty Marm dared to look around her at this peculiar new planet.

It was a bleak and lonely place, all black and grey, with damp air and very depressing scenery. As far as the eye could see, there were mountain ranges of grey and black. There was not one flower or green leaf, but there were trees of a sort – great forests of large, straight, grey trees, which seemed to be made of a rubbery kind of metal.

Old Noshie touched one of these trees and made a face – it had a very nasty stickiness.

"Look out!" yelled Skirty Marm. "Another earthquake!"

The ground was heaving again. The witches and Mendax were forced to cling to the nearest tree to stop themselves being shaken about like corks in a storm. Deep in the earth, far beneath their feet, there was a slow, rhythmic rumble.

"A tube train!" said Old Noshie knowingly – she had recently visited London.

"Don't be silly!" snapped Skirty Marm. "There's nothing like that here!"

Old Noshie scowled. "You don't know!"

"All right, smartie-stockings – where are the stations!"

The rumbling got louder. Mendax let out a "miaow" of fright. "Great heavens!" he gasped. "What a GHASTLY planet this is. No wonder Mrs A. ended up here!"

"Well, she can't have got the Glowing Stone yet," Skirty Marm said grimly, "or she'd have KILLED us ages ago."

"It's getting dark!" moaned Old Noshie. "I don't like it!"

Above them, the sky was whirling away from the orange glow of the distant sun. The strange landscape was plunged into sudden night, and the witches had to light the ends of their fingers to see anything (this does not hurt witches as it would a tender-skinned human).

"Noshie, stop that moaning," Mendax's cross voice mewed in the darkness. "I'd like to point out that this whole situation is your fault – you might at least try to be brave!"

"Shut up!" shouted Skirty Marm. "This is an emergency – we shouldn't be squabbling!"

Mendax sighed. "You're right. I shan't say one word about Old Noshie being a STUPID, SPROUT-COLOURED OLD NOODLE until we get home."

"Hey—" began Old Noshie furiously. But before she could insult the snooty little cat, the sky whirled once more, the ground heaved, and the whole planet was suddenly bathed in dazzling sunshine. The three magic friends saw each other's faces again, looking scared and extremely dirty – there was something very grubby and smeary about this place.

Skirty Marm glanced up at the horizon. Against the bright sky, she saw the outline of two jagged mountains. Terrible fear clawed into her soul – she did not know why, at first. Then it came to her all at once. The mountains were the exact same shape as Mrs Abercrombie's hideous nose and chin.

"This isn't a new planet at all!" she cried. "It's – it's – MRS ABERCROMBIE HERSELF!"

"What?" asked Old Noshie, deeply puzzled. "Where is she, then? What are you talking about?"

"Oh, don't be ridiculous!" mewed Mendax.

"If that's her nose and chin," Skirty Marm said, "we must be standing on her shoulder!"

The thought was disgusting. All three of them chorused, "YEUCH!"

"That stolen spell was so powerful," Skirty Marm went on, "that it's cloned Mrs A. from a tiny piece and grown her to half the size of our moon!"

"Dear me," Mendax said. "I shudder to think what all those underground noises are then."

"Of course!" Skirty Marm jumped excitedly on the squidgy ground. "That rumbling must be Mrs A. snoring – which means she's asleep, so we've got time to hide before she sees us!"

"Hide WHERE?" Old Noshie asked doubtfully.

"I'm sorry," Mendax mewed. "I refuse to go up her nose. Or in her ear."

Skirty Marm flung a skinny leg over her broomstick. "We'll fly into her hair – but remember, no sudden movements that might be itchy! One scratch, and we're all history!"

Mrs Abercrombie's hair lay beyond two mountain ranges. Old Noshie and Skirty Marm kept their brooms close to the ground. Knowing that the dreary landscape was Mrs Abercrombie made it look even uglier. It was not a pleasant flight. There were hills of flab, lakes of dribble, and warts the size of small castles.

To reach the thick grey forest of hair, they had to fly over Mrs Abercrombie's face. Old Noshie and Skirty Marm tried very hard not to look down, in case the repulsive sight made them faint and topple off their brooms. Mrs Abercrombie's nose was a steep crag that cast a huge shadow. They had to fly higher now to avoid the fierce gale blowing from her mouth and nose as she snored. They had to shut their eyes when the sun caught her metal teeth.

The witches landed at the top of Mrs Abercrombie's forehead and crept cautiously into her grey, tangled forest of hair. At every step they were terrified that the gigantic witch would wake and find them or (just as bad) suddenly scratch them off her head. Skirty Marm sat down against one of the trees, doing her best to forget that it was one of the old monster's hairs.

"If we manage to survive this," she announced, "I'm retiring – no more magical adventures. I've really had enough of magic now."

"Me too," agreed Old Noshie.

Mendax sighed. "I told Gingersnap I'd give up magic for ever if she'd marry me. I even told her I'd stop talking to humans."

"Ha! That'll be the day!" chuckled Old Noshie. "You couldn't stop talking if they made it illegal!"

Mendax coldly ignored this. "It was no use. Poor Gingersnap just couldn't believe that an innocent little country-cat like her could make me happy. I blame that brother of hers."

The last sentence was drowned by a long, deafening peal of thunder. Planet Abercrombie bucked and rolled until the witches and Mendax were bumped black and blue. Mrs Abercrombie had woken up. The sky was suddenly filled with a great, evil, familiar VOICE.

"I've grown again!" it roared. "When I get my Glowing Stone, I'll make them rue the day they threw ME off my throne! I shall crash into the miserable planet Earth, killing millions of stupid humans and making the rest into my SLAVES! Hahahaha! And every witch on Witch Island will bow down and worship me – not just as their QUEEN, but as their GOD! Hahahaha!"

The witches and Mendax stared at each other in despair. They had heard her plan. The whole Earth, and all the humans they knew and loved, were in mortal danger. And only two junior witches and one small cat stood between them and destruction. Though none of them dared to say it aloud, they all had the same thought: "We MUST try to save them – even if it KILLS us!"

"HahahahaHA!" laughed the shuddersome voice of Mrs Abercrombie.

"We can't do anything here," whispered Skirty Marm when the racket had died down. "Let's go!"

Mendax jumped into his basket. Old Noshie and Skirty Marm turned their rocket-brooms to full power. Flying away was a serious risk, especially now that Mrs A. was awake. Enormous as she was, she was bound to feel something when the flames shot out at take-off. Could they escape before she had time to notice them?

The brooms shot upwards into the grubby

grey sky of Planet Abercrombie. They were only just in time – as they zoomed through the atmosphere, an angry shout howled around them like a gale. The witches drove their brooms as fast as they could go and did not stop for a rest until they were several million miles away from Planet Abercrombie. Then they halted, on a globular cluster of stars near Jupiter.

Far away, through the mysterious universe, they saw a beautiful planet like a blue and green jewel.

"How pretty," said Old Noshie, "I should like to live there!"

"You DO live there, you goon," said Mendax. "It's EARTH." He let out a sob, which he turned into a cough. "Look at it, so calm and lovely! Imagine it smashed by that monster! What chance do we have to save it? We'll never find the Glowing Stone before she does!"

"Yes we will!" Skirty Marm said bravely.

Mendax shook his small, black head. "I must say, Skirty Marm, you impress me. Now that we are all about to die, I feel I should say how much I have always admired your plucky spirit. But even you have to admit, it's all impossible."

Skirty Marm was frowning her stubborn frown. She was not a witch who gave up easily. "That Glowing Stone used to be the Power Hat," she said thoughtfully. "And whatever it was, we never understood all its mysteries. But it has been very nice to us. I wish there was a way of asking it to help us now."

She sprang to her feet and startled Old Noshie by giving her a tremendous thump on the back. "Wait a minute – that's it!" she gabbled excitedly. "Don't you remember the way the Glowing Hat – I mean the Power Stone – hated Mrs Abercrombie? It burnt itself to ashes to stop itself going back to her! When it lived at Tranters End, it said it liked the humans and wanted to be GOOD!"

If cats had eyebrows, Mendax would have raised his. "So?"

"The Stone – or the Hat – works in ways that nobody understands," said Skirty Marm, breathless with excitement. "I'm going to try ASKING it to help us."

Mendax said sarcastically, "Do you have its phone number?"

"Quiet, cat," said Old Noshie, "unless you've got a better idea." She did not understand a word of the plan, but could not let Mendax take this lofty tone with her friend.

"That Stone can hear things," Skirty Marm said. "It can FEEL things and THINK things – even though everybody treats it like a box of tricks." She clenched her fists. "If I beg it to help the humans and the Earth, I really think it might listen!" She shut her eyes tight and concentrated harder than she had ever done in her life.

"This is ridiculous," snorted Mendax. "It'll never work."

"Shhhh," whispered Old Noshie. "Don't spoil it!"

The little cat shrugged rather scornfully. "Oh, well. What have we got to lose?"

"OW!" screamed Skirty Marm.

Something had stung the palm of her hand, very hard.

Old Noshie and Mendax stared as Skirty opened her hand to see what had hurt her. There, in her leathery palm, lay a jewel. It was a bit like a diamond, a bit like a pearl, and a bit like a drop of dew on a spider's web in the rising sun. It glowed with an eerie, silvery light. Mendax shaded his eyes with one paw, and Old Noshie's mouth hung open like a letterbox. This was incredible – Skirty's mad act of faith had worked. The wondrous Glowing Stone had heard her plea and travelled through space to find them.

Skirty Marm kissed it. "Oh, Stone! Thanks for coming!" She frowned rather anxiously. "Now, I wish I knew what to do with you!"

6

Battle in the Stars

Time on Earth and time in outer space move at very different rates. While the witches and Mendax were away, nearly a week had passed in Tranters End. Their human friends at the vicarage were dreadfully worried about them, but they had to pretend nothing was wrong – nobody else in the village had any idea that the wickedest witch in the world was on the rampage again.

Alice told anyone who asked that Old Noshie and Skirty Marm were visiting a friend on Witch Island.

Mr Snelling told people that Mendax was away at a Health Farm.

"I hate lying," he said miserably to Mr Babbercorn and Alice, "but nobody must guess what has happened. They've met Mrs Abercrombie, don't forget – they'd only be terrified, and what good would that do?"

Mr Babbercorn nodded sadly. "A panic is the last thing we need. We'll just have to carry on lying."

The tender-hearted vicar blew his nose. "I just wish," he said tearfully, "that I could say a few words of comfort to poor little Gingersnap. She's pining for my Mendax!"

Mr Snelling knew how Gingersnap felt. He missed Mendax too. On the sixth day of waiting and worrying, he went down to the Post Office and General Shop for some soap and a packet of cornflakes. This sort of shopping was usually done by Mendax, and Mr Snelling sighed as he thought of his beloved talking cat, pulling his small blue shopping-cart down the street.

Gingersnap was sitting on the post office windowsill. The romantic vicar thought he saw a look of lovelorn misery in her green eyes (female gingers are rare, and Gingersnap was very beautiful). Her silky, marmalade-coloured tail drooped sadly. Mr Snelling gave her a friendly stroke as he passed.

"Poor Ginger," said Mrs Tucker, "I know she's sorry she turned him down – I wonder if Mendax was right, and she let her brother bully her into it? She can't talk, but I could swear she understands every bit as much as Mendax!"

On his way out of the post office, the vicar halted beside Gingersnap. His round cheeks turned rather pink. He glanced up and down the street, to make sure nobody was watching, then he crouched down and muttered, "Look – er – Gingersnap – I've no idea how much you understand, or if what I'm saying sounds like gobbledegook – I mean, you're just an ordinary sort of cat (no offence). But let me assure you, Mendax still loves you! Please don't keep up this rubbish about you not being good enough. He loves you exactly as you are, and he wouldn't change you for the world!"

Was it his imagination, or did Gingersnap's ears twitch in a hopeful way? Mr Snelling felt a shade less miserable. He had set his heart on the two cats getting married and filling the vicarage with beautiful kittens. He wished more than ever that the three magic friends would come home safely, as soon as possible.

Apart from anything else, there was the problem of Mouldypage. The dusty old witch was staying in the spare bedroom at the vicarage. She was not easy to live with, treating them all like servants and asking for disgusting things to eat (for instance, mashed slugs in a cobweb gravy). Mouldypage refused to be kept hidden away, but liked to walk around the village, scaring people by suddenly glaring in at their windows. Alice was always having to apologize for her peculiar old guest. She explained that Mouldypage had done a cave-swap with Old Noshie and Skirty Marm while they were visiting Witch Island.

Mouldypage was very nosy and asked endless questions about human life. Why didn't humans

eat hedgehogs? Why were they always asleep at night? On the afternoon of the village Flower Show, Mouldypage wanted to know what was so special about flowers when you didn't eat them?

The people of Tranters End were well used to Old Noshie and Skirty Marm, and were very fond of them. But they did not know what to make of this grumpy, crusty, eccentric old witch in her sagging, holey purple stockings. She made them nervous when she told them she was nine hundred and eighty-seven years old and remembered the French Revolution "like it was yesterday".

The yearly Flower Show, which included the Marrow Cup, was held in a large, striped tent in the big field behind the vicarage. Outside the tent there were stalls selling tea and cakes, and a brass band ("Where are the Pock-horns?" asked Mouldypage). The day was warm and sunny, and the whole scene looked very festive.

Alice sighed, thinking how much the witches had loved their marrow. "If only they were here! If only they could see how beautifully their marrow has grown!"

"Yes," Mr Babbercorn smiled, a little sadly.

"We took such good care of it and wheeled it here in Thomas's buggy – it was the least we could do for them." He glanced at his watch, saw that it was time for Prizegiving and signalled to the vicar. Mr Snelling hastily finished his scone and stepped onto a wooden platform at one end of the tent. There was a public address system he had borrowed from the vicar of the next-door parish. It was very old, and it startled Mr Snelling when it squealed, "OO-EE-OO-EE-OO-EE!"

"Ladies and gentlemen," said the vicar into the microphone, once the squealing had died down, "welcome to the Tranters End Flower Show. As usual, it is my job to announce the prizes awarded by our judges. We begin with the Mrs Lumsden Book Token for Lupin of the Year—"

He was interrupted by a loud voice, crackling through the speakers on the platform.

"Hurry up, SLOWCOACH! What's the matter with that broom of yours!"

"Skirt!" shouted little Thomas, clapping his hands in delight.

"They're back!" cried Mr Snelling.

Skirty's voice came again. "We should be

down in Tranters End at any min— Aaargh! – WATCH OUT FOR THAT TENT!"

Above them, there was a tremendous ripping sound. Through the striped roof of the tent – smeared with dirt and smoking slightly – crashed Old Noshie, Skirty Marm and Mendax.

When Mouldypage saw the Glowing Stone and held it in her knobbly hand, all she would say for ages was, "Well, well, well!"

Witches, humans and cat watched her anxiously, waiting for the clever old witch to tell them what to do next. They had all slipped away from the Flower Show during the brass band's concert and were having a private conference in the vicar's study. Skirty Marm had told the humans of Mrs Abercrombie's evil plan, and they were all very pale and worried. Alice was holding Thomas very tight and looked as if she might cry.

"What can we do!" Skirty Marm asked impatiently. "How can we stop Mrs Abercrombie?"

"You must FIGHT her," Mouldypage croaked solemnly.

"What?" squeaked Old Noshie. "Fight HER?

Just the three of us?"

Mouldypage was stern. "Just ONE of you, for it is written in the Great Parchment that the last battle must be single combat." She shot out her tongue and swallowed a passing bluebottle. "Normally, I'd say you didn't stand a chance. But you have the Glowing Stone and it seems to like you. It might decide to obey you, even if you can't put commands into the correct code."

She held up the stone. It filled the room with its soft, eerie, silver light. "Who is it to be?"

"ME," said Skirty Marm bravely.

"Oh, no!" wailed Old Noshie. "It should be ME because this is all my fault!"

"I too am filled with a sense of noble self-sacrifice," Mendax said heroically, "but I'll try not to let it lead me into doing something foolish. Skirty Marm is obviously the best witch for the job."

"Thanks, cat," said Skirty Marm. She shuddered. Even when armed with the Glowing Stone, facing Mrs Abercrombie alone was a terrifying prospect.

"Oh, Skirty, please—" begged Alice. "Be careful!"

"What shall I do if she EATS you?" sobbed

Old Noshie. "I can never manage without you!"

"Skirty, we're all very proud of you," said Mr Babbercorn. "Be as brave as you can. Remember that the Glowing Stone is so beautiful because it is so GOOD – and that goodness must always beat wickedness in the end!"

"Bleuch!" shouted Mouldypage. "Stop this revolting human SLUSH! Prepare to send out your challenge!"

She pressed the Glowing Stone into Skirty Marm's hand.

"But I haven't a clue what I'm supposed to do with it!" cried Skirty Marm.

"Tell it what you want – and get going!" shouted Mouldypage.

"All right," Skirty Marm said bravely. She turned to the others, trying to keep the wobble out of her voice. "This is goodbye, then."

"I'm coming with you!" cried Old Noshie. "I'm not going to be left out of your last adventure!"

Mendax was already fitting on his space helmet. "All for one, and one for all," he mewed. "Vicar, if I don't come back – be KIND to Gingersnap!"

"I will!" promised Mr Snelling.

Their broomsticks were propped up outside the back door. The witches mounted – Old Noshie still sobbing and moaning, Skirty Marm grimly silent. Mr Babbercorn helped Mendax into his basket on the back of Old Noshie's broom.

Skirty Marm clutched the Glowing Stone and concentrated with all her might. "Stone, I don't know the right way to ask you, but this is an emergency. Take me to where I can have my final battle with Mrs A.!"

All at once, the world seemed to turn upside down. The witches just had time to hear Alice screaming, and Mouldypage saying "Whoops!", before they found themselves zooming somewhere beyond the Milky Way.

Old Noshie did not like being in outer space. She was just thinking how lonely it all was, when she realized Mendax was miaowing frantically behind her.

She looked over her shoulder to see what was the matter and yelled, "Oh NO!"

With a shaking hand, she pushed the radio-switch on her broom. "Skirt! Something awful's happened! We've got Mr Babbercorn!"

It was all too true. Dangling from Mendax's

basket was the limp, pale form of the weedy young curate.

"Oh, STOCKING-STITCH!" Skirty Marm swore furiously, looking round. "He'll die up here! Glowing Stone – for goodness sake – do something!"

Hovering in mid-space, the witches and Mendax watched breathlessly. Mr Babbercorn moaned and coughed, then began to breathe normally. The Glowing Stone had made him his own private atmosphere. He opened his eyes, and they nearly popped out of his head when he found himself clinging to the back of a broomstick in the middle of uncharted space.

"Am I dreaming?" he murmured.

"Sorry about this," said Skirty Marm, riding her broom alongside him. "You got caught up by mistake. We'd better take you home."

"Certainly not," said Mr Babbercorn boldly. "Now that I'm here, I'm staying. I wouldn't miss this for the world."

The Glowing Stone suddenly became beautifully warm in the palm of Skirty Marm's hand. She looked down at it, and was surprised to see it shining with a soft, pinkish light.

"Mr B.," she said slowly, "I think the Stone

brought you here on purpose!"

"It always did like you," Old Noshie agreed (Mr Babbercorn had once worn the Glowing Stone when it had taken the form of a woolly bobble hat for a while).

"We don't know what it's planning," said Mr Babbercorn, "but we know it's on our side!"

They all felt braver now, and more cheerful. Skirty Marm saw a large lump of rock nearby with a nice flat surface, and signalled to Old Noshie to land. They dismounted, and disentangled Mr Babbercorn from Old Noshie's broom. Once he had got over the shock, Mr Babbercorn found outer space fascinating. He discovered that he could jump enormous distances across the flat rock, sending up a shower of sparkling dust every time he landed. He could leap hundreds of feet off the ground. Something in the special air he was breathing made him feel incredibly strong. He felt he could have picked up an office block and hurled it a hundred miles.

Then, suddenly, he knew why he was there.

"Witches," he said, very gravely, "I think the Glowing Stone wants ME to fight Mrs Abercrombie."

The witches and Mendax gasped, astounded.

"But you're a human!" protested Old Noshie. "You'll never be able to fight her!"

"I'm ready now," said Mr Babbercorn bravely. "Far readier than Skirty Marm – the Stone has prepared me."

Skirty scowled. She could never let the curate face Mrs Abercrombie alone. "Rubbish!" she snapped. "Mrs A. would make mincemeat of you!"

Mr Babbercorn's face was full of determination and dignity, although his clothes were covered with stardust and his glasses were hanging off by one ear. He put them back on his nose. "If you don't believe me, ask the Glowing Stone!"

They all stared at the Stone, lying in Skirty Marm's hand. As they watched, it slowly turned from silvery white to a deep, soft crimson – then there was a sudden flash of red light around the curate's head.

Skirty Marm gasped. "You're right – it is you it wants!"

She was offended that the Glowing Stone thought she wasn't tough enough to fight Mrs Abercrombie, but she was also secretly relieved that she didn't have to.

"Please give the Glowing Stone to me," Mr Babbercorn said. He took it, and held it up. "Thanks for choosing me," he said to it. "Please give me a weapon."

A few sparks fizzed in his hand. Then they grew into long rays of white light, almost too bright to look at. These dazzling spears twisted themselves into a sword in Mr Babbercorn's hand. He waved the sword and leapt gracefully upwards. It was an amazing sight – one that the witches and Mendax would never forget. Mr Babbercorn was hopping through the sky, using stars as stepping stones. And with each hop, he grew, until he was as gigantic as Mrs Abercrombie.

He landed on a meteorite, and his voice was huge enough to make the whole universe ring.

"Mrs Abercrombie, I challenge you to single combat, to the DEATH! Come and fight me, if you DARE!"

"Are you calling me a COWARD?" roared the dreadful voice of Mrs Abercrombie. "We'll see about that!" Her terrible voice was inside their heads. It was all around them, filling the whole universe – it was everywhere.

Something bright was rushing through the sky towards them. Mendax and the witches huddled together in terror when they saw it was the vast form of Mrs Abercrombie.

A ball of fire shot out of her mouth, and screamed straight at Mr Babbercorn. His friends trembled, but he made his sword into a cricket bat and whacked the fireball straight back at Mrs Abercrombie. It hit her on the bottom, and she howled with pain and rage. This time a fiery eagle, four times the size of Mr Babbercorn, leapt out of her mouth. It rushed at Mr Babbercorn to tear him apart with its great claws of fire. Old Noshie wailed and covered her eyes. Skirty Marm turned ghostly pale, and Mendax shook like a leaf.

But Mr Babbercorn stood firm. He held up his silver sword. The monstrous, flaming eagle swooped down on him and its scorching breath was close enough to singe the curate's eyebrows.

"I have a bird more powerful than that!" Mr Babbercorn called to her.

He sliced through the darkness and neatly cut off the eagle's head. It changed into a silver dove, shining with a light that was very bright and extremely beautiful. The witches and

Mendax each felt that they could gaze at that silver dove for ever.

The effect upon Mrs Abercrombie was very different. She was very angry, of course. But there was something else. Her face turned the colour of the skin on porridge, and her mean beady eyes widened in sheer disbelief.

"I don't believe it!" muttered Mendax. "She's SCARED!"

"How can she be scared of that beautiful bird?" wondered Old Noshie.

Skirty Marm's piercing red eyes had been watching intently. "She knows that Mr B. and the Stone are working together as a team – it's obeying his THOUGHTS as soon as he has them. Mrs A. always had to cast complicated spells before she could get it to do anything!"

Mr Babbercorn climbed on to the back of the outsized silver dove, brandishing his silver sword like a Knight of the Round Table.

"You can't beat us," he said, in a great voice like calm thunder. "The Glowing Stone – which you TRAPPED in your power by making it into the Power Hat – has no intention of being a hat AGAIN. It has chosen me to fight for it, because I am a clergyman and it's my job to help it to be GOOD."

"NO!" screamed Mrs Abercrombie, in rage and anguish. "It's not true! You're lying! That Stone respects me for my brains! It admires me for my wickedness! Ever since I made it into my Power Hat, it has WORSHIPPED me as its QUEEN! I'll destroy you all! And I'll start with your STINKY LITTLE FRIENDS!"

"Witches – Mendax – take cover!" called Mr Babbercorn. They dived behind a boulder, just in time to shelter from a storm of enormous rocks and shooting stars. Mrs Abercrombie screeched with annoyance when her missiles failed to kill them.

"You've RUINED my Stone!" she screamed, in a towering passion. "You took it to live with the humans, and you turned it soppy and useless!"

"SURRENDER!" Mr Babbercorn cried. "Your days of evil are over!"

"Never – OW! What's going on?" the enormous, planet-sized, horrible face of Mrs Abercrombie went grey with fright and disbelief. "How DARE you?"

Old Noshie, Skirty Marm and Mendax began to laugh – Mr Babbercorn's magical sword had

begun to shoot out long ribbons of light that zipped through the sky and wound themselves around Mrs Abercrombie like strands of sticky jelly. Soon, she was wrapped up like a huge, wriggling cocoon.

"I won't let you kill her," Mr Babbercorn said to the Glowing Stone. "I want you to find a way of trapping her until the very End of Time! I want you to programme her so that if she ever comes near our lovely Earth again, she will disintegrate into a million pieces!"

Before their astonished eyes, the magical sword hopped out of Mr Babbercorn's hand, turned itself into the biggest tennis racket that has ever been seen and whacked the trapped Mrs Abercrombie thousands of miles across the universe before neatly turning itself into a sword again. They watched, with open mouths and gaping eyes, as Mrs Abercrombie's jelly-covered figure disappeared into the far distance.

The sword returned to Mr B.'s hand and was a Stone again – pale and flickering, as if it were exhausted.

The friends from Earth all stood in the vast, humming quiet of the skies.

Old Noshie was the first to speak. "Where did she go?"

Mr Babbercorn took off his glasses and cleaned them with his handkerchief. "The Stone tells me she is trapped, for Eternity, in one of the rings of Saturn – going round and round, like a bundle of clothes in a washing machine. She won't be bothering us again." He laughed suddenly. "Not even if Old Noshie buys another illegal spell!"

This time, thanks to the kindness of the Glowing Stone, time had been altered so that the Flower Show was still going on when Mr Babbercorn and the magic trio arrived back in Tranters End. Everyone in the village now knew what had happened, and they burst into loud cheers when the broomsticks crashed to the ground in the big field.

There were hugs and kisses, and explanations. The villagers rushed to their homes to bring food and drink for a big, impromptu party. Once they realized that the evil Mrs Abercrombie was defeated and the Earth was safe, all they could think of was celebration.

"Witches," said Mrs Tucker, "I'd just like to say, it was a great day for Tranters End when the two of you came to live in our belfry." (There were cries of "Hear hear!" from the other villagers.) "We've had a few shocks and upsets, but you've taught us all that witches and humans can be the best of friends."

"Three cheers for Old Noshie and Skirty Marm!" shouted someone. "Three cheers for the Belfry Witches!"

Old Noshie and Skirty Marm were overcome. All they could do was smile and blush and bow their heads. It was a wonderful moment.

Mr Snelling stepped forward. "And now, the final Prize. Because of their hard work, and everything they've done for us – and just because we love them so much – the judges have decided to award the Tranters End Marrow Cup to Old Noshie and Skirty Marm!"

He handed the grand silver cup to Old Noshie. She had dreamed of putting it in the belfry, and now she glowed like a green traffic light with the sheer joy of it.

"You've all been so kind to us," Skirty Marm said, in an unusually shaky voice. "Me and Nosh are proud to belong to this lovely village. But I do think we've forgotten one thing." She turned to Mr Babbercorn. "May I have the Glowing Stone?"

Mr Babbercorn gave it to her. She cradled the Stone very gently in the palm of her hand.

"This is who – or WHAT – we have to thank," she said. "When I first knew this Stone, it was the Power Hat, and I thought it was wicked. I now know it was in Mrs Abercrombie's power then, and that it really wants to be very good. Stone, I have one last command for you – tell us something that we can do for YOU!"

The Glowing Stone suddenly shot out a glorious rainbow of lights. Like a hissing gust of wind, a great, sighing voice filled the air around them.

I have waited thousands of years for this moment — the moment I could ASK to be set free! If you set me free, I can go back where I belong — to the Hills Before Time!

"Well, off you go, then," said Skirty Marm, patting it. "And thanks for everything."

The wind fell silent. The Glowing Stone was gone. Skirty Marm and Old Noshie heaved big sighs of relief.

"I didn't like to say anything in front of it," Skirty Marm said, "but I'm glad to see the back of that Stone — it's caused nothing but trouble! Now both it and Mrs A. are history, we can all get on with living happily ever after!"

And that is exactly what they did. Old Noshie and Skirty Marm led a busy life in Tranters End — dabbling in mild magic, but staying off the heavy stuff. They had both had enough of adventures and thought their village the best place in all the universe. Surprisingly, Mouldy-page agreed with them. The strange old witch retired from the State Library and bought an old shed in the woods outside Tranters End. She did not come into the village much, but pottered about contentedly among her books.

Mendax proposed to Gingersnap again, and this time she accepted. To the delight of Mr Snelling, they got married and produced a litter of five beautiful kittens – two ginger boys, and three little black girls. They all began life by mewing in the normal way, but it soon became clear that they could understand and speak English.

"They can speak cattish to their mother, and personish to their father," Mr Snelling would explain proudly to flabbergasted strangers who had heard the kittens singing along to their nursery rhyme tape.

"I believe I'm the happiest and luckiest cat in the world!" Mendax declared one day, when he and Mouldypage were having tea with Noshie and Skirty in the belfry. Inevitably, they fell to talking about Witch Island (now a dull but peaceful place), and the bad old days of the queen.

"We're definitely the happiest and luckiest witches," said Old Noshie, gulping down a live bat.

"Yes, it was a great day for us when we got

infected with nasty human habits," said Skirty Marm teasingly, winking at Old Noshie and Mendax. "All that niceness, and kindness, and kissing and hugging—"

"And being helpful," said Old Noshie.

"And telling the TRUTH," added Mendax.

Mouldypage puffed calmly at her pipe. "Maybe it's not so bad," she muttered.

"Yes," said Skirty Marm, laughing, "those soppy human customs are the best ones, after all!"

Kate Saunders
BELFRY WITCHES 1
A Spell of Witches

Old Noshie and Skirty Marm have committed a terrible crime. They've
sung a frightfully rude song about Mrs Abercrombie, Queen of the
Witches, at the Hallowe'en Ball. Now they are to be banished from
Witch Island for ever!

Where can two wacky witches find a new home? The sleepy village of
Tranters End is about to get a bewitching surprise . . .

Kate Saunders
BELFRY WITCHES 2
Mendax the Mystery Cat

Old Noshie and Skirty Marm have been trying terribly hard to be good.
They've only done the tiniest bit of magic, they haven't touched a drop
of Nasty Medicine, and they've even been learning how to knit!

But strange powers are at work in Tranters End. First there's the
underwear that comes to life, then the flying pigs – and then a very
mysterious black cat arrives at the vicarage door . . .

Kate Saunders
BELFRY WITCHES 3
Red Stocking Rescue

Old Noshie and Skirty Marm are terribly upset. Although they've promised to be good, Mr Babbercorn won't let them be bridesmaids at his wedding. And Mendax the cat isn't even allowed to sing a solo!

But then deep, dark magic turns Alice, Mr Babbercorn's bride-to-be, into a snail. Who is the culprit – and can two brave witches (and one clever cat) cook up a spell that will save the wedding from disaster?

Kate Saunders
BELFRY WITCHES 4
Power Hat Panic

Tranters End is full of excitement. A rich and mysterious old lady has moved into a ruined cottage in the woods, and now she's buying everyone presents.

But Old Noshie and Skirty Marm aren't fooled. This creepy creature may look like a sweet old granny, but she's none other than their worst enemy – monstrous Mrs Abercrombie, Queen of the Witches. And she's come to reclaim her Power Hat . . .

Collect all the BELFRY WITCHES books!

The prices shown below are correct at the time of going to press. However, Macmillan Publishers reserve the right to show new retail prices on covers which may differ from those previously advertised.

All Macmillan titles can be ordered at your local bookshop or are available by post from:

Book Service by Post
PO Box 29, Douglas, Isle of Man IM99 1BQ

Credit cards accepted. For details:
Telephone: 01624 675137
Fax: 01624 670923
E-mail: bookshop@enterprise.net

Free postage and packing in the UK.
Overseas customers: add £1 per book (paperback)
and £3 per book (hardback).